Robin and the Silver Arrow

Tales of Robin Hood

First published in 2006 by
Franklin Watts
338 Euston Road
London
NW1 3BH

Franklin Watts Australia
Hachette Children's Books
Level 17/207 Kent Street
Sydney
NSW 2000

A CIP catalogue record for this book is available from the British Library.

ISBN (10) 0 7496 6689 7 (hbk)
ISBN (13) 978-0-7496-6689-7 (hbk)
ISBN (10) 0 7496 6703 6 (pbk)
ISBN (13) 978-0-7496-6703-0 (pbk)

Series Editor: Jackie Hamley
Series Advisor: Dr Barrie Wade
Series Designer: Peter Scoulding

Printed in China

Franklin Watts is a division of
Hachette Children's Books.

Robin and the Silver Arrow

by Damian Harvey and Martin Remphry

The Sheriff of Nottingham was very pleased. He'd thought of a way to catch Robin Hood.

The Sheriff had decided to hold an archery tournament. He was sure Robin would want to prove he was the best archer in the country.

And when he did, the Sheriff would catch him!

News of the tournament soon reached Sherwood Forest.
"The winner gets a silver arrow," said Much.

"I'll win that arrow," said Robin.

"No!" cried Will Scarlet,

"I'm sure it's a trap."

But Little John had an idea.

"Let's go in disguise," said Little John. "Robin can wear gold, Will can wear pink and I'll go in blue. No one will recognise us."

"Yes," laughed Robin. "And when we get there, we can borrow the Sheriff's soldiers' uniforms. He won't be looking out for his own soldiers!"

The day of the tournament arrived and crowds of people came. Robin's merry men soon found some uniforms to borrow.

The Sheriff and his soldiers kept
a lookout for Robin Hood.
“He must be here!” said the Sheriff.

The archers lined up and took their first shots. Thud! Thud! Thud!

Many arrows hit their targets and the crowd cheered. Anyone who missed was out of the tournament.

The targets were moved further back and the archers fired again.

Thud! Thud! Thud!

Soon, only Robin Hood and one of the Sheriff's soldiers were left.

The soldier fired and his arrow landed near the centre of the target.

Then Robin fired.

Thud! His arrow landed right in the centre.

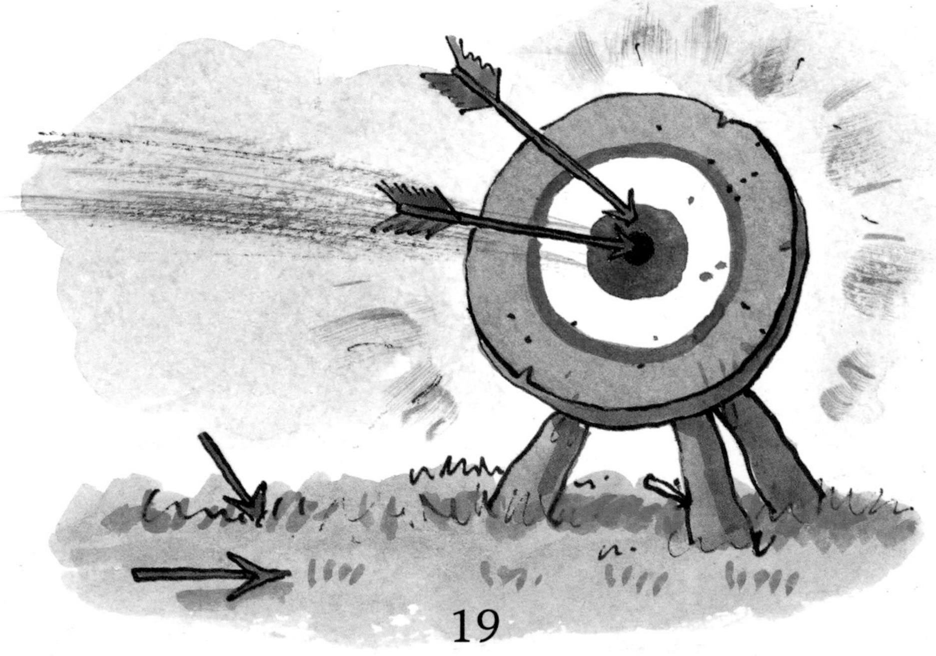

The soldier's second shot landed right next to Robin's arrow. Robin took careful aim and fired his last arrow.

Thwak! Robin split the soldier's arrow in two. A huge cheer came up from the crowd. Robin had won!

"Ah ha!" said the Sheriff as he handed over the silver arrow. "There's only one person in England who can shoot like that … Robin Hood. Arrest him!"

There was no escape for Robin.
The soldiers grabbed him.

"Not so fast," cried Little John. "Let Robin go or you'll need to find yourselves a new sheriff."

Robin and his merry men escaped back to Sherwood Forest and took the Sheriff with them.

If the soldiers came too close, one of Will's arrows sent them running.

Robin thanked the Sheriff for helping them escape, then sent him back to Nottingham …

... but only after Little John had

taken his jewels!

"I don't think the Sheriff will ever forget the name of the best archer in England," laughed Little John. "It's Robin Hood!"

Hopscotch has been specially designed to fit the requirements of the National Literacy Strategy. It offers real books by top authors and illustrators for children developing their reading skills. There are 37 Hopscotch stories to choose from:

Marvin, the Blue Pig
ISBN 0 7496 4619 5

Plip and Plop
ISBN 0 7496 4620 9

The Queen's Dragon
ISBN 0 7496 4618 7

Flora McQuack
ISBN 0 7496 4621 7

Willie the Whale
ISBN 0 7496 4623 3

Naughty Nancy
ISBN 0 7496 4622 5

Run!
ISBN 0 7496 4705 1

The Playground Snake
ISBN 0 7496 4706 X

"Sausages!"
ISBN 0 7496 4707 8

The Truth about Hansel and Gretel
ISBN 0 7496 4708 6

Pippin's Big Jump
ISBN 0 7496 4710 8

Whose Birthday Is It?
ISBN 0 7496 4709 4

The Princess and the Frog
ISBN 0 7496 5129 6

Flynn Flies High
ISBN 0 7496 5130 X

Clever Cat
ISBN 0 7496 5131 8

Moo!
ISBN 0 7496 5332 9

Izzie's Idea
ISBN 0 7496 5334 5

Roly-poly Rice Ball
ISBN 0 7496 5333 7

I Can't Stand It!
ISBN 0 7496 5765 0

Cockerel's Big Egg
ISBN 0 7496 5767 7

How to Teach a Dragon Manners
ISBN 0 7496 5873 8

The Truth about those Billy Goats
ISBN 0 7496 5766 9

Marlowe's Mum and the Tree House
ISBN 0 7496 5874 6

Bear in Town
ISBN 0 7496 5875 4

The Best Den Ever
ISBN 0 7496 5876 2

ADVENTURE STORIES

Aladdin and the Lamp
ISBN 0 7496 6678 1 *
ISBN 0 7496 6692 7

Blackbeard the Pirate
ISBN 0 7496 6676 5 *
ISBN 0 7496 6690 0

George and the Dragon
ISBN 0 7496 6677 3 *
ISBN 0 7496 6691 9

Jack the Giant-Killer
ISBN 0 7496 6680 3 *
ISBN 0 7496 6693 5

TALES OF KING ARTHUR

1. The Sword in the Stone
ISBN 0 7496 6681 1 *
ISBN 0 7496 6694 3

2. Arthur the King
ISBN 0 7496 6683 8 *
ISBN 0 7496 6695 1

3. The Round Table
ISBN 0 7496 6684 6 *
ISBN 0 7496 6697 8

4. Sir Lancelot and the Ice Castle
ISBN 0 7496 6685 4 *
ISBN 0 7496 6698 6

TALES OF ROBIN HOOD

Robin and the Knight
ISBN 0 7496 6686 2 *
ISBN 0 7496 6699 4

Robin and the Monk
ISBN 0 7496 6687 0 *
ISBN 0 7496 6700 1

Robin and the Friar
ISBN 0 7496 6688 9 *
ISBN 0 7496 6702 8

Robin and the Silver Arrow
ISBN 0 7496 6689 7 *
ISBN 0 7496 6703 6

*** hardback**